THIS
LITTLE
LIGHT-ME

*Teaching Your Child and Yourself to
Have Self Esteem - No Matter What*

1st Edition

Elizabeth Wiley

Trafford rev. 11/04/2021

www.trafford.com
North America & international
toll-free: 844-688-6899 (USA & Canada)
fax: 812 355 4082

INTRODUCTION

Our books are written as on ongoing series for high risk youth, veterans, and first responders as well as their parents and those who are raising them.

One of the reasons for starting this series was we, as special needs teachers, as therapists, as Directors of programs and private schools for high risk youth began to recognize how many of the children and youth were children of veterans, grandchildren of veterans, and also first responders.

We then noticed the numbers of minority children and poverty level financial back grounds were the reality for high risk children and youth. We saw children of Mothers who had been as young as NINE at the birth of their child among the high risk students. Whether rich, or poverty level, we saw children of alcohol, sexual, and drug addictions.

We saw children as young as 18 months labeled with an alphabet of mental health disorders, medicated and put into "special schools" where in fact media found they were often warehoused, abused, and not taught at all. Upon seeing a news story about the schools discovered at some of the licensed sites, in which children and teens often did not have desks, or chairs to sit on, let alone proper educational supplies and equipment for special learning program, we joined with others, and designed programs.

We were naive enough to think our work, offered FREE in most cases, would be welcomed especially as we offer it free and often through research projects, but, it was NOT valued or wanted.

What? we asked?

We went back to college and while earning degrees we had apparently NOT needed while working with children of the very rich in expensive private schools, we did research projects to document our findings. To find ways to overcome the problems. Again, our work was NOT valued or wanted.

One of our associates, who had asked many of us to volunteer in a once a month FREE reading program in the local public schools, was held back for almost two years doing paperwork and proving her volunteers, most of them parents of successful children, teens and adults, could read a first five years book and teach parents how to read those books to their own children. She was a Deputy United States Prosecutor, and had recruited friends from all levels of law enforcement, child and family services, education and volunteer groups that served children and families.

None the less, we continued our work, met a fabulous and expensive Psychiatrist who was building his own server system and the first online education project after creating a massive and encompassing medical examination study guide for graduate medical students to assist them in passing global and national medical examinations for licensing.

We worked with a team of citizens and specialists in education who had created a 39 manual project for students, parents and teachers to be able to learn on their own.

This series of books includes ideas, history and thoughts from the students, the parents, and professionals who work with these situations.

Jesus was told, don't have children wasting your time, and he responded, let the children come.

Our work is to bring children to us, and to those who have the heart and love to develop the uniqueness and individuality of each of God's creations. Many of them are of different religions, and beliefs, and many are atheists but believe fully in the wonder and uniqueness of every human.

To all who have helped and continue to help children and anyone wanting to learn, we thank God and we thank you.

This little light: Me

In our programs, we start each meeting with an introduction of ourselves, and go around the room: I am ....and I am wonderful because God created me, there will never be another me.

When a baby is born, do we greet that child with JOY.

Were we GRATEFUL even before the child is born and in our arms?

That feeling of JOY is going to transmit to the baby, before birth, and as it is clipped free of the natal cords and blood lines.

If we greet that child, wanted or unwanted at first, with JOY, our own feeling of JOY is going to be hardwired into the neurology of the child. This prenatal and natal caring and concern are subject of many research projects over the years of how attitude, music, stress change the neurological responses of the unborn. Every person needs to research this BEFORE having sex, and risking a child being unwanted. IF you do not want children, don't have sex, OR use birth control, OR get permanent birth control surgery.

SO, getting started starts BEFORE your child is even out in the air!

excerpted from our accompanying book JOY.

IMPORTANT DAILY REMINDER:

From the day your child is born, remind yourself not to let your own light be dimmed, and make a commitment not to let anything or anyone dim your child's light.

History, as it really is, not what we are told to believe by any one country, or culture to fit into THEIR agenda, shows humans spend a lot of time feeling NOT OK. Today it is big business to identify, label and medicate the NOT OK. Few programs spend time teaching each person to recognize their own worth, and unique "light" in this world.

Being a parent makes it YOUR job to not only find your own "light" and make it shine, but to help your child to find their "light" and make it shine, no matter outward circumstances.

Many commercials are funny, heart felt, and give us good information. Others try to make the not OK think their product will make their consumers OK. Teach your children not to think any "thing" is going to make them OK. You will save your child many hours of bad feelings about themselves due to not having the "right" products.

Find pictures of "lights"

draw or paste some here......talk with your children, what kind of light are you

Can we change light type from time to time? Draw with them what this looks like. Talk about how our light seems when we are happy. When we are sad. When we are helping someone we love. Discuss other times you light might change. Draw some of these lights.

Chapter One

. . . .

From the day your child is born, remind yourself not to let your own light be dimmed, and make a commitment not to let anything or anyone dim your child's light

Bible: Matthew 5:15 Let your light shine

History, as it really is, not what we are told to believe by any one country, or culture to fit into THEIR agenda, shows humans spend a lot of time feeling NOT OK. Today it is big business.

LET YOUR LIGHT SHINE

Matthew 5:16 So that others may see your light, light your light and keep it lit to Glorify God.

Each of us is given a gift. Working with some famous politicians and celebrities, I have met many who have lit their lights, but sadly darkly, Working with some of the top 1% brains and scientists in the world I learned that many of them are very incomplete and unhappy. Doing some hands on science projects with science graduate students, and some very disabled students, I saw and learned that each of us has a gift, and it helps make the lights of others shine.

Asking Graduate science students from all over the world to design projects that met the needs of their own children for hands on understanding of major problems in their own countries. (I volunteered in the Diversity Department during off hours in my own Department, or as part of a project for our Department Pre- College Education designed to unify science education because the two founders of the Department had been complaining about the need to take one or two years to bring all the science students up to the same speed in their science understanding and ability after starting college level science programs which only took the top science students from any country to begin with. They said, "Someone" should, and then "why not us", and stopped complaining and put together teams to address the problems globally. I learned that the graduate students KNEW the science, math, engineering, but did not KNOW the science, math or engineering from a standpoint of joy and application to real life. Teaching small children and teens locally helped the world's top graduate students apply their math with the joy the children and teens found in those sciences.

Little children in foster group homes, probation special ed programs, and physically challenged children, often with Down's Syndrome or Cerebral Palsy or major birth defects that left them without the physical capability to BE educated taught these top science students to be LOVED, not just the students and graduate students, all learned what COULD be done, and to love science, not just the math, and formulas, but the things they learned in hands on programs helped even the top graduate students see possibilities in the reality of the science.

Between them, the graduate students learned to LOVE not just the students assigned to them, but science, math and engineering as well. The students in the special needs groups helped us ALL to just have "joy" in our lives. They also often asked questions which helped us all learn what the real question was in the projects the students were assigned in their graduate level programs, and HOW to enjoy the process, not just feel anger and not OK by the world's refusal to think about some of the premises. We each need to let our light shine, it just might be the light needed to help someone else see, to help the whole world work together to resolve problems.

Children in these programs when asked about pollution: said "don't litter". If every corporation and person in this world had that simple thought in mind, no matter what they were doing.......drinking a drive through soda and throwing the cup out the window, or designing a corporation that had a ZERO carbon footprint system for poison or garbage left from their processes....WOW, what a wonderful world we could have.

PICK UP LITTER: Again, a child, thrown away by society because of inability to function at even a failing grade level in public schools, and not admitted into private academic schools had told us all the answer. WHAT if we spent all the money we spend in hating and fighting and political battles over pollution paying teams of graduate science students to take on one single project for a corporation and help them clean it up.

The graduate students asked, how do we pay for it. The kids, remember these are thrown away discarded kids of our academic masters, said "charge a little more for the items. Most of us pay taxes on anything we purchase, we pay the two dollars more for gas as the prices increase, what would a penny or ten pennies more on anything mean if it means NO pollution of air, water, dirt, and NO danger to employees and customers of the products. No destruction of nature and animals! If it means every corporation, city, county, state and all nations committed to have the research done, and the projects started, or even completed in ninety days........BIG promises for thirty to fifty years from now are useless.

Chapter Two

. . . .

My Light

Parents need to let their own light shine before they put out the light of their children's light.

BIG promises for thirty to fifty years from now are useless.

IF parents crush the light of their children, trying to make them meet the wishes and dreams of the parent (s) what was the purpose.

How often do we see children struggling and hating education because the parent(s) want the child to have the education the parent did not have.

Children need to go to school. They need to learn the basics of reading, writing, math, science, and other arts, they need to recognize all of the sciences as art forms, They need to learn to respect and honor everyone.

Parents work two jobs, and are too tired to play with, or love their children. They think they are loving their children. Many a parent says "MY" child will be the first college graduate, or graduate student, or doctor, scientist or engineer, baker, candlemaker, or politician. IS it what your child wants to become.

Take a careful look at what you "think" your child wants. If it is really something YOU want, write it down and begin a process of making that YOUR dream, it is NOT your child's dream. Whether "good" or "bad" your dreams of your childhood and teens were long past, and not for a complete child today.

Many teens, today, and. even children commit suicide or are taking drugs, drinking and 'rebelling' against the enforced dreams of a long ago child or teen dream of their parent(s).

For example: BUY your teen that new, super car you thought you wanted at sixteen. Your child is going to become immediately attractive to others who do NOT have that vehicle, not because those people care for your teen, but because they want access to that vehicle.

It is hard enough for a teen who can not understand why their friendships and relationships are shallow and fail, it is because the people they attract are people who want access to that vehicle NOT because they care about your teen, but a teen is hurt in heart and soul, blaming themselves for not being cared for and loved loyally. YOU were the one who wanted that vehicle as a teen. You can afford to buy one now, for you, and if it is the twenty year old classic YOU wanted, your child's user pals are NOT going to be excited by it!

Make a list of all those things YOU wanted that you are forcing on your child. The list is more than likely LONG. Go over the list with your spouse, parents, a community or religious leader and figure out what is GOOD for your child, and what is just YOUR long gone child or teen forcing the life right out of your child.

Chapter Three

. . . .

MY light, I won't let anyone PFFT it out

How did you let YOUR light get PFFT out?

When you were a child, or a teen, you had dreams, did YOU learn to choose carefully, and that dreams take work, dedication, sacrifice?

Or were you just told NO, take MY dreams from parents, teachers, and others until your own light went out, or puttered?

Today, as an adult, do you stand up for YOUR dreams, YOUR thoughts, YOUR best person? or do you let the great "they" in commercials, movies, music, and pressure of ads tell you what or who YOU want to be?

SHUD is a four letter word.

Learn not to tell others what they SHUD do, it puts out their light. Learn not to let others tell you what you SHUD do, it puts out your light. Jesus told us, honor God, believe Jesus when he says, believe and have faith and repent sincerely and God will give you forgiveness. If GOD can forgive us, we certainly forgive others and they can forgive us for SHUDDING.

List ways that Pfft your light out: Addictions are a big area of letting your light be snuffed out. Whether drugs, alcohol, overeating, bulimia, anorexia, overspending, driving unsafely, over exercising, being lazy, workaholism, gossiping, being more involved in celebrity lives, or television show lives than your own family......all of these are addictions, and there are many others. Over picky, too much cleanliness is an addiction. Have you ever gone to someone's house for dinner and they are pulling the dishes out from under your fork to wash them? Criticizing others (especially disguised as "I just want to help you) is an addiction........

List other addictions or ways YOU have to blow out your light, to turn or dim the switch on your light, or the lights of your spouse, children or family and friends? How can YOU change YOUR behavior. Can you apologize and let everyone shine more brightly?

Chapter Four

Let is not the same as MAKE your child's light shine

Take a careful look at your own life: DID YOU learn from those who forced you or did you learn from those who showed you the path and LET your light shine on that path?

Make a list of the ways in which YOU were MADE to do things, rather than allowed to let your own light shine? How did that affect your life? If you keep that pain, anger and bitterness, how do you think it will affect your child? What can you do to forgive those who MADE you, rather than let you, shine YOUR light? How can you rekindle YOUR light rather than try to force YOUR light to shine on putting out the lights of your children?

. . . .

Chapter Five

Put it under a bush, NO

Many parents try to teach their children to "help" others. This is a good thing, IF done with proper balance.

Love others AS yourself, not more, not less.

Matthew 22: 37-39

When asked by his apostles what the law was, Jesus told them Love and Honor God, and Love others AS yourself, not more, not less.

Many people have been taught, and teach their children that this means to love (or not love, but give things)to others MORE than they love themselves. This can be putting your light under a bush, because it makes you and/or your children unhappy.

This does NOT mean that we always have to give up things we want, for things others need. If you put your own light OUT trying to keep someone else afloat, you are NOT helping yourself, or the other person. It does mean, sometimes we DO make the CHOICE to give up something we want, to give something to someone else who NEEDS it.

List ways you put your own light under a bushel rather than light it. How can you still care for others without putting out your own light.

List ways you put your child's light under a bush. How can you change this. Discuss this with your child and family.

Chapter Six

. . . .

Let YOUR Light shine.....

Matthew 5; 16.
Let YOUR light shine
to reflect Glory to God

Many people appear to have been taught
that if they let their light shine, be joyful, or
enjoy life, they are not sacrificing enough to
reflect Glory to God.

Jesus, through Matthew 5:16 tells us to LET
our LIGHT SHINE.

What does YOUR light shining mean to you?
Being a good parent? Being a good spouse?
Being a good child. Being a good friend?

*Being a good member of the community?
Sometimes just a smile and handshake, or a
plate or bag of food to someone on the block
is your light shining brightly.*

Make a list, with your children, of things you can do to make your light shine brightly.

What are small things that make your light shine? Some examples are: do not litter. If you take a walk, or go to the park, or the beach, or any recreation area, take along some small grocery bags and pick up trash that you can leave in the trash can at the park, or beach. Put your shopping cart back, ask an elderly or disabled person, or a person with children if you might put their cart back for them. Look around, ask if you might help someone unload a heavy item from the cart into the vehicle. Pay for the person in front of you or behind you in the market, or somewhere. We do this, and just say, pass it along to someone else...... it translates to every language, age and culture. I have asked kids if I might pay for the items in their pocket, I have noticed they planned to steal them, but by offering to pay for them, they have to bring them out and I pay for them. Hopefully it takes a message Oof not stealing and forgiveness along. Kids, look around and take all your papers, litter, and toys OUT of the car when you get home. Offer to carry things in, instead of just rushing off to play with the toys you whined to get while your parent was shopping. Don't whine for toys. Make a list and save your own money, or do chores at home or for relatives to earn the money to pay for them

Our family list:

Chapter Seven

Let YOUR light shine in the community, school, and on the block

The more we let OUR light shine, the more we encourage the lights of others to shine, we might even light someone's light by our actions.

Look around and be part of community projects. Some are more fun than others, but YOU can make even the less fun projects MORE fun by smiling, and bringing along snacks and drinks to share.

Many of our veterans have disabilities that make it hard for them to do some of the projects, but we ask them to come and hand out the big garbage bags, and give out name tags and drinking water. One of our favorite seniors likes to go and bring back the food. We ask for donations, and she figures out what we can buy for all the people attending a river cleaning day, or a park cleaning day, or a mountain cleaning day. Beach and desert cleaning days can be planned with tents, and over nights with big local groups, or even bigger groups that use the beaches, or come up to the desert or mountains for recreation.

Raise money. You might not be a great runner, so plan a walk......it was fun to be one of those with crutches walking along with wheelchair elders and veterans and being part of a 5K marathon to make commitments to better each of our own selves.....all those people figuring out what that meant for themselves and raising support from friends and relatives to buy the shirt and get a good start helped each of us start, and keep on going.

Find out what your school or city needs, and create a way to make it happen. While recycling is not at a high during Covid, in some states it is mandatory for any store that sells recyclable materials and collects the fees to have a recycling station on their property. YOU can make sure this is starting up again. Even if you ask most people to donate the recyclable items to something for the city or schools, YOU can help get a new recycling station at least once a week and give coupons for the store instead of cash, finding a couple of family members with trucks to cash in the recyclables and turn in the money to build a new skate park, or repair an old one, to clean up the basketball, tennis, or other sports areas. To clean up and put in new equipment on disc gold courses for public use...This is a good sport because it does NOT require taking out the natural plants, and requires every player to learn and stick to good rules of using the trails and facilities.

Cities have taken the cost of a huge community pool set up, and broken it down to how many cans it will take to build it, and raised those funds. In large areas, it was as few as 100 cans per person over the six months or year of fundraising. The recycling plants will usually bring out a huge container attached to a truck to gather the cans, bottles, and plastic, then send a *check to the fundraiser. It actually saves them money to not have to deal with full time staff at a recycling station.*

Include everyone. Ask restaurants to donate two or four meal coupons, and raffle them for bags of recycling. If children in your area need warm or better clothing, ask a huge thrift store, veterans, or others, to give a one hour training on pricing, and ask everyone to bring in washed, cleaned and BAGGED (who does not have several grocery bags to donate for the sale)items. Ask food trucks to come in for two or three hours and donate a percentage of their profit for that time period. It is FREE advertising for them. MANY stores, if asked, have clothing and shoes they have taken off the shelves and will donate to a community yard sale for a donation receipt. Many restaurants will donate five gallon drink containers and their own soft drink glasses for a donation receipt. THEIR accountants take care of the paperwork and THEY get FREE advertising.

Chapter Eight

. . . .

Address big issues

Bullying is a big issue: Crime, drunk driving, shop lifting (while a crime is not always seen as one that costs all of us money), graffiti.

When the whole community turns on ITS lights to shine on the problems, they are resolved easier, faster and better. List some big issues you can shine light on.

There was a great group of O L D people who raised their own money, bought little folding chairs, and bought some shirts at a local discount tee shirt shop, the shirts were seconds and had the word CARE on them, so the seniors decided to call their project, Grandparents CARE. They worked with the school, and bus companies to put seniors in the front and rear of each bus. Lonely seniors who no longer could drive had a nice day and got to know the kids, they also were part of the orientation the KIDS thought up to get cooperation to make sue everyone had a safe, and non-bullied ride to and home from school.

The kids loved their Grandparents, and protected them. More than once we heard someone, usually a previous bully, say, HEY, don't bother him/her.....they help us. We love them. These lovely people sat in their chairs along the routes home with cell phones to called the police if necessary To provide a safe spot for the children, both parents and kids knew these volunteers, they were from their own blocks, or the blocks they had to walk to and from school. These Grandparents sat one outside in the hall, and one in the doorway of the big bathrooms in the schools, This let the kids and parents feel safe for their children to go to the bathroom, and it ended the bullying and vandalism of the bathrooms.

Many parents had children and teens who were criminals, and harmed the community. The Grandparents helped other parents to ask the parents for a talk to ask them if they could help get that child more on track for a better outcome in school and life. The parents were asked to be part of the solution, NOT treated like the spawners of the devils. The youth were asked to be part of the solution for ALL KIDS, and the neighborhood, not just "fix themselves".

Make a list with your spouse, your children, your neighbors on how you ALL can shine your lights together until the problems are resolved.

The Community needs things. When youth and criminals become part of the neighborhood, they stop hurting the community. Especially when you ask them to help figure out what to do!!!

Skate parks, skate board half pipes and swimming pools, with a couple of basketball courts and neighborhood teens and college students hired to do safety training and sell juice and healthy snacks (popcorn, low fat chips, and fruit) hello all the kids and have jobs.

This is another great place for grandparents and the disabled to sit with their dogs, and talk to the kids. They also have phones to call the police if needed. Paramedics, police, and fire personnel often swim, skate, and skateboard, and are a good community addition to this type of neighborhood improvement if they come and volunteer to talk about safety and first aid. An important part is to have the youth raise the money themselves. In a school district with 10,000 students, with help from community building projects (such as Habitat for Humanity who will sometimes consider a recreational area community project) can figure out the price for math classes. They can find out how to do the business requests for donations and help as English and other projects for credit. AND raise money with other community groups. Give local churches, temple, mosques and Scout or Camp Fire or Path finder programs special dates in exchange for helping raise the money needed. Classrooms can figure out how many cans, and bottles need to be brought in by each child, and get some parents, or grandparents with trucks to take them to recycling. Some huge projects can ask the city or private recycling programs to bring in dumpsters, and pay for filled loads. The youth, in math class can figure out how much the city is spending on graffiti and vandalism repair and help the city council realize they actually will SAVE MONEY by building community WITH their youth in their own neighborhoods.

Community groups raise money. HELP THEM help you. Whether calendars, cookies, crafts, raffle tickets, wreaths you can make a deal and help them for a donation for your project.

ASK the community what they can do. A licensed swimming pool contractor can be asked for a great deal on a large community pool for all ages. Cement and other contractors can, and do offer discounts for a tax deduction for the materials which further reduces the cost of the project.

PLANT TREES and prepare the parking strips for homeowners to plant gardens of their choice on each block. If all the plants are bought in bulk, the project can ask nurseries to give donations, and/or discounts for tax deductions. The nurseries know they are going to interest more local people in gardening.

You can make YOUR light shine by helping others brighten up their lights.

Chapter Nine

. . . .

Keeping MY light shining, Letting my Child keep their light shining

Now that I know that it is important to keep MY light shining, I will LET, not FORCE my child keep their light shining.

List some things below I can do each day to keep my light shining.

List some things below I can do each day to LET my child's light shine (and remember, even over sixty, your child is still your child, and does NOT need all your helpful advice and criticism. It might be hard to learn, but sometimes your job, for yourself, and your child to keep on shining, is to shut up!

List some ways to help my whole family SHINE more each day.

These things can include your extended family, and neighbors. You can all talk about a monthly thank you to people we all fail to thank.

Buy a small flower bouquet for the house. Have the florist drop off a nice bouquet for nurses at a nursing home, the patients out for physical therapy will enjoy them as well. Have a crafts kit donation day for every classroom in your district and donate them to nursing homes, children's group homes, children's long term hospital classrooms...... veteran art centers at the VA hospital. Your light will be glowing!

We asked classrooms to make place mats for veterans in hospitals. AND to buy a nice card or two for the hospitalized veterans to send to THEIR family and friends for birthdays, and upcoming holidays with a roll of stamps. The Social Worker started crying when she saw what the cities children had done for "her vets". The veterans loved the placemats so much, they hung them on their walls by. their beds instead of using them on the holiday trays!

Make your neighborhood shine. We asked parolees, and gang members to join in making the neighborhood's cleaner, safer and more involved. We even asked police, fire, and paramedics to block clean ups. Making neighborhoods makes all lights shine more.

Buy a donut, or a dozen cookies for the next holiday, raise money if you do not have enough to pay for two or five, or twenty dozen really great treats to be delivered to the neighborhood people who help us live better, but we forget about them. The sanitation, water, sewer, gas, electric and. cell tower workers. The hospital or school maintenance staff, Those who clean sports and entertainment centers.

Fire Departments, police departments and paramedics dress up and deliver presents to many all over the City. Ask them what they need, and donate nice items for them to give. These first responders often have to help children when parents are injured or killed in accidents or crimes a snuggly blanket, and toy to give to children waiting for relatives, or Family Services to come pick them up is always appreciated by both the children and first responders.

Chapter Ten

....

Closing

Closing and Other Books by Author and team

Closing:

All of our group of books, and workbooks contain some work pages, and/or suggestions for the reader, and those teaching these books to make notes, to go to computer, and libraries and ask others for information to help these projects work their best.

To utilize these to their fullest, make sure YOU model the increased thoughts and availability of more knowledge to anyone you share these books and workbooks with in classes, or community groups.

Magazines are, as noted in most of the books, a wonderful place to look for and find ongoing research and information. Online search engines often bring up new research in the areas, and newly published material.

We all have examples of how we learned and who it was that taught us.

One of the strangest lessons I have learned was walking to a shoot in downtown Los Angeles. The person who kindly told me to park my truck in Pasadena, and take the train had been unaware that the weekend busses did NOT run early in the morning when the crews had to be in to set up. That person, being just a participant, was going much later in the day, taking a taxi, and had no idea how often crews do NOT carry purses with credit cards, large amounts of cash, and have nowhere to carry those items, because the crew works hard, and fast during a set up and tear down and after the shoot are TIRED and not looking to have to find items that have been left around, or stolen.

As I walked, I had to travel through an area of Los Angeles that had become truly run down and many homeless were encamped about and sleeping on the sidewalks and in alleys. I saw a man, that having worked in an ER for many years I realized was DEAD. I used to have thoughts about people who did not notice people needing help, I thought, this poor man, this is probably the most peace he has had in a long time. I prayed for him and went off to my unwanted walk across town. As I walked, I thought about myself, was I just heartless, or was I truly thinking this was the only moment of peace this man had had for a long time and just leaving him to it. What good were upset neighbors, and police, fire trucks and ambulances going to do. He was calmly, eyes open, staring out at a world that had failed him while alive, why rush to disturb him now that nothing could be done.

I did make sure he was DEAD. He was, quite cold rigid.

I learned that day that it is best to do what a person needs, NOT what we need.

Learning is about introspection and grounding of material. Passing little tests on short term memory skills and not knowing what it all means is NOT education, or teaching.

As a high school student, in accelerated Math and Science programs, in which I received 4.0 grades consistently, I walked across a field, diagonally, and suddenly all that math and science made sense, it was not just exercises on paper I could throw answers back on paper, but I realized had NO clue as to what it all really meant.

OTHER BOOKS BY
THIS AUTHOR, AND TEAM

Most, if not all, of these books are written at a fourth grade level. FIrst, the author is severely brain damaged from a high fever disease caused by a sample that came in the mail, without a warning that it had killed during test marketing. During the law suit, it was discovered that the corporation had known prior to mailing out ten million samples, WITHOUT warnings of disease and known deaths, and then NOT telling anyone after a large number of deaths around the world started. Second, the target audience is high risk youth, and young veterans, most with a poor education before signing into, or being drafted into the military as a hope Many of our veterans are Vietnam or WWII era.

Maybe those recruiting promises would come true. They would be trained, educated, and given chance for a home, and to protect our country and its principles. Watch the movies Platoon, and Born on the Fourth of July as well as the Oliver Stone series on history to find out how these dreams were meet.

DO NOT bother to write and tell us of grammar or spelling errors. We often wrote these books and workbooks fast for copyrights. We had learned our lessons about giving our material away when one huge charity asked us for our material, promising a grant, Instead, we heard a couple of years later they had built their own VERY similar project, except theirs charged for services, ours were FREE, and theirs was just for a small group, ours was training veterans and others to spread the programs as fast as they could. They got a Nobel Peace prize. We keep saying we are not bitter, we keep saying we did not do our work to get awards, or thousands of dollars of grants....but, it hurts. Especially when lied to and that group STILL sends people to US for help when they can not meet the needs, or the veterans and family can not afford their "charitable" services. One other group had the nerve to send us a Cease and Desist using our own name. We said go ahead and sue, we have proof of legal use of this name for decades. That man had the conscience to apologize, his program was not even FOR veterans or first responders, or their families, nor high risk kids. But we learned. Sometimes life is very unfair.

We got sued again later for the same issue. We settled out of Court as our programs were just restarting and one of the veterans said, let's just change that part of the name and keep on training veterans to run their own programs. Smart young man.

Book List:

The Grandparents Story list will add 12 new titles this year. We encourage every family to write their own historic stories. That strange old Aunt who when you listen to her stories left a rich and well regulated life in the Eastern New York coastal fashionable families to learn Telegraph messaging and go out to the old west to LIVE her life. That old Grandfather or Grandmother who was sent by family in other countries torn by war to pick up those "dollars in the streets" as noted in the book of that title.

Books in publication, or out by summer 2021

Carousel Horse: A Children's book about equine therapy and what schools MIGHT be and are in special private programs.

Carousel Horse: A smaller version of the original Carousel Horse, both contain the workbooks and the screenplays used for on site stable programs as well as lock down programs where the children and teens are not able to go out to the stables.

Spirit Horse II: This is the work book for training veterans and others interested in starting their own Equine Therapy based programs. To be used as primary education sites, or for supplementing public or private school programs. One major goal of this book is to copyright our founding material, as we gave it away freely to those who said they wanted to help us get grants. They did not. Instead they built their own programs, with grant money, and with donations in small, beautiful stables and won....a Nobel Peace Prize for programs we invented. We learned our lessons, although we do not do our work for awards, or grants, we DO not like to be ripped off, so now we copyright.

Reassessing and Restructuring Public Agencies; This book is an over view of our government systems and how they were expected to be utilized for public betterment. This is a Fourth Grade level condemnation of a PhD dissertation that was not accepted be because the mentor thought it was "against government". The first paragraph noted that a request had been made, and referrals given by the then White House.

Reassessing and Restructuring Public Agencies; TWO. This book is a suggestive and creative work to give THE PEOPLE the idea of taking back their government and making the money spent and the agencies running SERVE the PEOPLE ;not politicians. This is NOT against government, it is about the DUTY of the PEOPLE to oversee and control government before it overcomes us.

Could This Be Magic? A Very Short Book. This is a very short book of pictures and the author's personal experiences as the

Hall of Fame band VAN HALEN practiced in her garage. The pictures are taken by the author, and her then five year old son. People wanted copies of the pictures, and permission was given to publish them to raise money for treatment and long term Veteran homes.

Carousel TWO: Equine therapy for Veterans. publication pending 2021

Carousel THREE: Still Spinning: Special Equine therapy for women veterans and single mothers. This book includes TWELVE STEPS BACK FROM BETRAYAL for soldiers who have been sexually assaulted in the active duty military and help from each other to heal, no matter how horrible the situation. publication pending 2021

LEGAL ETHICS: AN OXYMORON. A book to give to lawyers and judges you feel have not gotten the justice of American Constitution based law (Politicians are great persons to gift with this book). Publication late 2021

PARENTS CAN LIVE and raise great kids.

Included in this book are excerpts from our workbooks from KIDS ANONYMOUS and KIDS JR, and A PARENTS PLAIN RAP (to teach sexuality and relationships to their children. This program came from a copyrighted project thirty years ago, which has been networked into our other programs. This is our training work book. We asked AA what we had to do to become a real Twelve Step program as this is considered a quasi twelve step program children and teens can use to heal BEFORE becoming involved in drugs, sexual addiction, sexual trafficking and relationship woes, as well as unwanted, neglected and abused or having children murdered by parents not able to deal with the reality of parenting. Many of our original students were children of abuse and neglect, no matter how wealthy. Often the neglect was by society itself when children lost parents to illness, accidents or addiction. We were told, send us a copy and make sure you call it quasi. The Teens in the first programs when surveyed for the outcome research reports said, WE NEEDED THIS EARLIER. SO they helped younger children invent KIDS JR. Will be republished in 2021 as a documentary of the work and success of these projects.

Addicted To Dick. This is a quasi Twelve Step program for women in domestic violence programs mandated by Courts due to repeated incidents and danger, or actual injury or death of their children.

Addicted to Dick 2018 This book is a specially requested workbook for women in custody, or out on probation for abuse to their children, either by themselves or their sexual partners or spouses. The estimated national number for children at risk at the time of request was three million across the nation. During Covid it is estimated that number has risen. Homelessness and undocumented families that are unlikely to be reported or found are creating discussion of a much larger number of children maimed or killed in these domestic violence crimes. THE most important point in this book is to force every local school district to train teachers, and all staff to recognize children at risk, and to report their family for HELP, not punishment. The second most important part is to teach every child on American soil to know to ask for help, no matter that parents, or other relatives or known adults, or unknown adults have threatened to kill them for "telling". Most, if not all paramedics, emergency rooms, and police and fire stations are trained to protect the children and teens, and get help for the family. PUNISHMENT is not the goal, eliminating childhood abuse and injury or death at the hands of family is the goal of all these projects. In some areas JUDGES of child and family courts were taking training and teaching programs themselves to HELP. FREE.

Addicted to Locker Room BS. This book is about MEN who are addicted to the lies told in locker rooms and bars. During volunteer work at just one of several huge juvenile lock downs, where juveniles who have been convicted as adults, but are waiting for their 18th birthday to be sent to adult prisons, we noticed that the young boys and teens had "big" ideas of themselves, learned in locker rooms and back alleys. Hundreds of these young boys would march, monotonously around the enclosures, their lives over. often facing long term adult prison sentences.

The girls, we noticed that the girls, for the most part were smart, had done well in school, then "something" happened. During the years involved in this volunteer work I saw only ONE young girl who was so mentally ill I felt she was not reachable, and should be in a locked down mental health facility for help; if at all possible, and if teachers, and others had been properly trained, helped BEFORE she gotten to that place, lost in the horror and broken of her childhood and early teen years.

We noticed that many of the young women in non military sexual assault healing programs were "betrayed" in many ways, by step fathers, boyfriends, even fathers, and mothers by either molestation by family members, or allowing family members or friends of parents to molest these young women, often as small children. We asked military sexually assaulted young women to begin to volunteer to help in the programs to heal the young girls and teens, it helped heal them all.

There was NOTHING for the boys that even began to reach them until our research began on the locker room BS theory of life destruction and possible salvaging by the boys themselves, and men in prisons who helped put together something they thought they MIGHT have heard before they ended up in prison.

Americans CAN Live Happily Ever After. Parents edition. One Americans CAN Live Happily Ever After. Children's edition Two. Americans CAN Live Happily Ever After. Three. After Covid. This book includes "Welcome to America" a requested consult workbook for children and youth finding themselves in cages, auditoriums on cots, or in foster group homes or foster care of relatives or non-relatives with NO guidelines for their particular issues. WE ASKED the kids, and they helped us write this fourth grade level workbook portion of this book to help one another and each other. Written in a hurry! We were asked to use our expertise in other youth programs, and our years of experience teaching and working in high risk youth programs to find something to help.

REZ CHEESE Written by a Native American /WASP mix woman. Using food, and thoughts on not getting THE DIABETES, stories are included of a childhood between two worlds.

REZ CHEESE TWO A continuation of the stress on THE DIABETES needing treatment and health care from birth as well as recipes, and stories from Native America, including thoughts on asking youth to help stop the overwhelming numbers of suicide by our people.

BIG LIZ: LEADER OF THE GANG Stories of unique Racial Tension and Gang Abatement projects created when gangs and racial problems began to make schools unsafe for our children.

DOLLARS IN THE STREETS, ghost edited for author Lydia Caceras, the first woman horse trainer at Belmont Park.

95 YEARS of TEACHING:
A book on teaching, as opposed to kid flipping Two teachers who have created and implemented systems for private and public education a combined 95 plus years of teaching talk about experiences and realities and how parents can get involved

in education for their children. Included are excerpts from our KIDS ANONYMOUS and KIDS JR workbooks of over 30 years of free youth programs.

A HORSE IS NOT A BICYCLE. A book about pet ownership and how to prepare your children for responsible pet ownership and along the way to be responsible parents. NO ONE needs to own a pet, or have a child, but if they make that choice, the animal, or child deserves a solid, caring forever home.

OLD MAN THINGS and MARE'S TALES. this is a fun book about old horse trainers I met along the way. My husband used to call the old man stories "old man things", which are those enchanting and often very effective methods of horse, pet, and even child rearing. I always said I brought up my children and my students the same as I had trained horses and dogs......I meant that horses and dogs had taught me a lot of sensible, humane ways to bring up an individual, caring, and dream realizing adult who was HAPPY and loved.

STOP TALKING, DO IT

ALL of us have dreams, intentions, make promises. This book is a workbook from one of our programs to help a person make their dreams come true, to build their intentions into goals, and realities, and to keep their promises. One story from this book, that inspired the concept is a high school kid, now in his sixties, that was in a special ed program for drug abuse and not doing well in school. When asked, he said his problem was that his parents would not allow him to buy a motorcycle. He admitted that he did not have money to buy one, insure one, take proper driver's education and licensing examinations to own one, even though he had a job. He was asked to figure out how much money he was spending on drugs. Wasting his own money, stealing from his parents and other relatives, and then to figure out, if he saved his own money, did some side jobs for neighbors and family until he was 18, he COULD afford the motorcycle and all it required to legally own one. In fact, he did all, but decided to spend the money on college instead of the motorcycle when he graduated from high school. His priorities had changed as he learned about responsible motorcycle ownership and risk doing the assignments needed for his special ed program. He also gave up drugs, since his stated reason was he could not have a motorcycle, and that was no longer true, he COULD have a motorcycle, just had to buy it himself, not just expect his parents to give it to him.

Printed in the United States
by Baker & Taylor Publisher Services

Printed in the United States
by Baker & Taylor Publisher Services